Just Like You

Jan Fearnley

To the memory of my father, Leslie Robertson.

He was very, very special.

And for his grandchildren, David and Elizabeth.

Love and thanks to Genevieve and Ramona.

EGMONT
We bring stories to life

First published in Great Britain in 2000
This edition published in 2014 by Egmont UK Limited
The Yellow Building, 1 Nicholas Road, London W11 4AN
www.egmont.co.uk

Text & illustrations copyright © Jan Fearnley 2000
Jan Fearnley has asserted her moral rights
ISBN 978 1 4052 7269 8

A CIP catalogue record for this title is available from the British Library.

EGMONT LUCKY COIN

Our story began over a century ago, when seventeen-year-old Egmont Harald Petersen found a coin in the street.
He was on his way to buy a flyswatter, a small hand-operated printing machine that he then set up in his tiny apartment.
The coin brought him such good luck that today Egmont has offices in over 30 countries around the world.
And that lucky coin is still kept at the company's head offices in Denmark.

Stay safe online. Any website addresses listed in this book are correct at the time of going to print.
However, Egmont is not responsible for content hosted by third parties. Please be aware that online content
can be subject to change and websites can contain content that is unsuitable for children.
We advise that all children are supervised when using the internet.

It was dusk. The red evening sun snuggled down to the hillside, resting on purple pillows of clouds. Mama Mouse and Little Mouse were making their way home to bed.

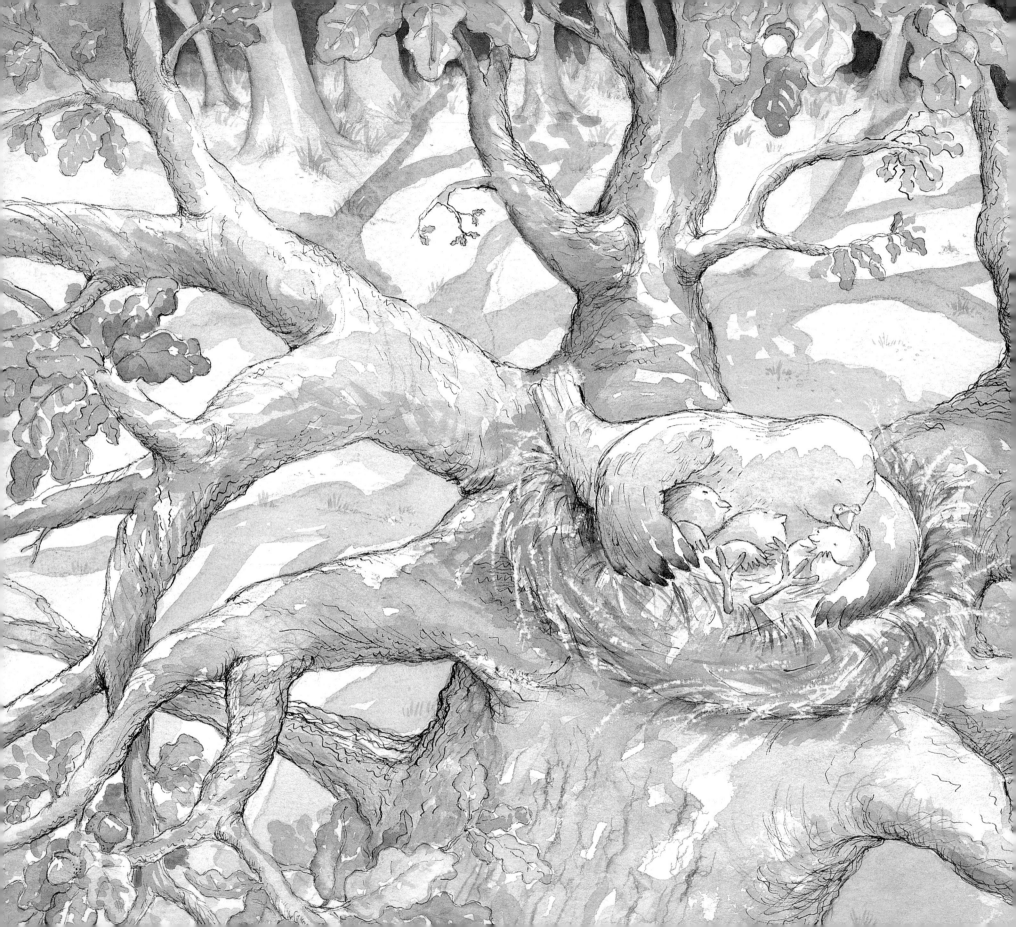

As they walked along, they could hear the other animals
talking quietly to their babies as they settled them down
for the night. Mama Bird was tucking her chicks into the
nest. Carefully, tenderly, she smoothed their downy feathers.

"I will fly for you," she sang softly as they closed their little eyes.
"I will fly as high as the clouds, across the skies, to find the
finest food for you. That's what I will do."

"Isn't that lovely," said Little Mouse.

"Her babies must be very special."

"Yes, they are," said Mama Mouse.

"Just like you."

They came upon Daddy Frog.

He was tucking his froglets under a lilyleaf.

"I will jump for you," he told them.
"I'll jump as high as the sky and bring
you the juiciest bugs. That's what I will do."

"I'm not sure about the bugs," said Little Mouse,

"but his babies sound very special too."

"They certainly are," said Mama Mouse.

"Just like you."

As they tiptoed through the grasses, they came upon
Mama Rabbit with her kittens, catching the last of the sunshine.

"I will dig for you," she told them. "I will dig the deepest,
most secret burrow to keep you safe as treasure and warm forever.
That's what I will do."

"That's a lot of hard work," sighed Little Mouse.

"What special, special babies."

"Just like you," said Mama, squeezing his little paw.

As they walked along the seashore, they could
make out the sound of Mama Seal crooning to her pup.
They were settled on a bed of weeds as the waves lapped
a lazy lullaby against the shore.

"I will swim for you, my darling,"
she said. "I will dive as deep
as the deepest ocean, and find you
the sweetest of treasures: shells,
corals and fish, whatever you wish.
That's what I will do."

"Verrrry special," sighed Little Mouse.

"Just like you," reminded Mama.

But Little Mouse had a faraway look about him.

Wandering up the hillside, they saw Fox playing with his cubs.

"I will run for you," he said. "I will run as far and as fast as ever
I can and be clever and quick and cunning to keep you safe from harm.
That's what I will do."

Little Mouse looked very thoughtful.

Now they were home.

Mama Mouse gave her baby,

Little Mouse, a cuddle.

"It's time for bed," she said.

As he got ready, Little Mouse looked at his Mama
and said, "Mama, what will *you* do for *me*? You can't fly,
or jump high, you don't dig or dive and you can't run as fast as
a fox. You're only a little mouse. Am I not as special, then?"

Mama Mouse smiled and
tucked her baby under the covers.
"Well, all that may be true," she said,
"but even a little mouse can do quite
a few things. Let me see . . .

I'll tell you stories to make you smile,

I'll find you nice things to nibble on,

I'll play with you and
make you laugh,

I'll hug you and keep you safe and . . .

. . . when you're naughty, I promise I'll be very, very cross with you!

But most of all, I promise I will always love you and
care for you. And I'll do it with all of my heart."

Little Mouse smiled a sleepy smile.

"That's an awful lot. I must be very,

very special," he said.

"Yes, you are," whispered Mama,

dropping a kiss on his little furry head.

And as Mama Mouse tiptoed to the bedroom door,

Little Mouse whispered, "Just like you, Mama. Good night."